Dear Parent:

Buckle up! You are about to join your child on a very exciting journey. The destination? Independent reading!

Road to Reading will help you and your child get there. The program offers books at five levels, or Miles, that accompany children from their first attempts at reading to successfully reading on their own. Each Mile is paved with engaging stories and delightful artwork.

Getting Started
For children who know the alphabet and are eager to begin reading
• easy words • fun rhythms • big type • picture clues

Reading With Help
For children who recognize some words and sound out others with help
• short sentences • pattern stories • simple plotlines

Reading On Your Own
For children who are ready to read easy stories by themselves
• longer sentences • more complex plotlines • easy dialogue

First Chapter Books
For children who want to take the plunge into chapter books
• bite-size chapters • short paragraphs • full-color art

Chapter Books
For children who are comfortable reading independently
• longer chapters • occasional black-and-white illustrations

There's no need to hurry through the Miles. Road to Reading is designed without age or grade levels. Children can progress at their own speed, developing confidence and pride in their reading ability no matter what their age or grade.

So sit back and enjoy the ride—every Mile of the way!

D0057520

For the New York Yankees
In memory of Leslie A. Schade
1905-1999

Library of Congress Cataloging-in-Publication Data
Schade, Susan.
Cat at Bat / by Susan Schade and Jon Buller.
    p.   cm. — (Road to reading. Mile 2)
Summary: Cat manages to help her team win a close baseball game.
ISBN 0-307-26211-1 (pbk) — ISBN 0-307-46211-0 (GB)
[1. Animals Fiction. 2. Baseball Fiction. 3. Stories in rhyme.]
I. Buller, Jon. II. Title. III. Series.
PZ8.3.S287Cag 2000
[E]—dc21   99-24651
                                                  CIP

A GOLDEN BOOK • New York
Golden Books Publishing Company, Inc. New York, New York 10106

ISBN: 0-307-26211-1 (pbk)   A MM
ISBN: 0-307-46211-0 (GB)

Cat at Bat

by Susan Schade and Jon Buller

"Let's play ball!"
say Cat and Rat.

Skunk has the gloves.

Bee has the bat.

Turtle can catch,

and Chick can slide.

Rabbit can hit

from either side.

The Orange Blossoms
play to win.
They loosen up.

The fans crowd in.

Batter up!

The pitch is low.

Cat doesn't swing.

She lets it go.

STRIKE ONE! the call.

STRIKE TWO!

STRIKE THREE!

Three strikes—you're out!

It's up to Bee.

But Bee strikes out,

and so does Rat.

And then the Sharks
come up to bat.

The Sharks are good.
They hit. They score.

Late in the game
they lead five-four.

The Blossoms take
their last at bat.

A walk!

Two hits!

Then up comes Cat.

The pitcher glares.

He makes Cat wait.

Cat paws the dirt.

She taps home plate.

The pitch.

The swing.

A loud...

THA·WAACK!

She tumbles over
on her back.

Cat gets a hit—
a giant one.

It's going! It's gone!
GRAND-SLAM HOME RUN!

Cat picks her hat
up off the ground.

She dusts her rump.

She trots around.

The Blossoms win it,
eight to five!

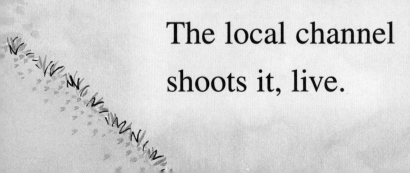

The local channel
shoots it, live.

Win or lose,
Cat loves to play.
It's ice cream after,
either way.